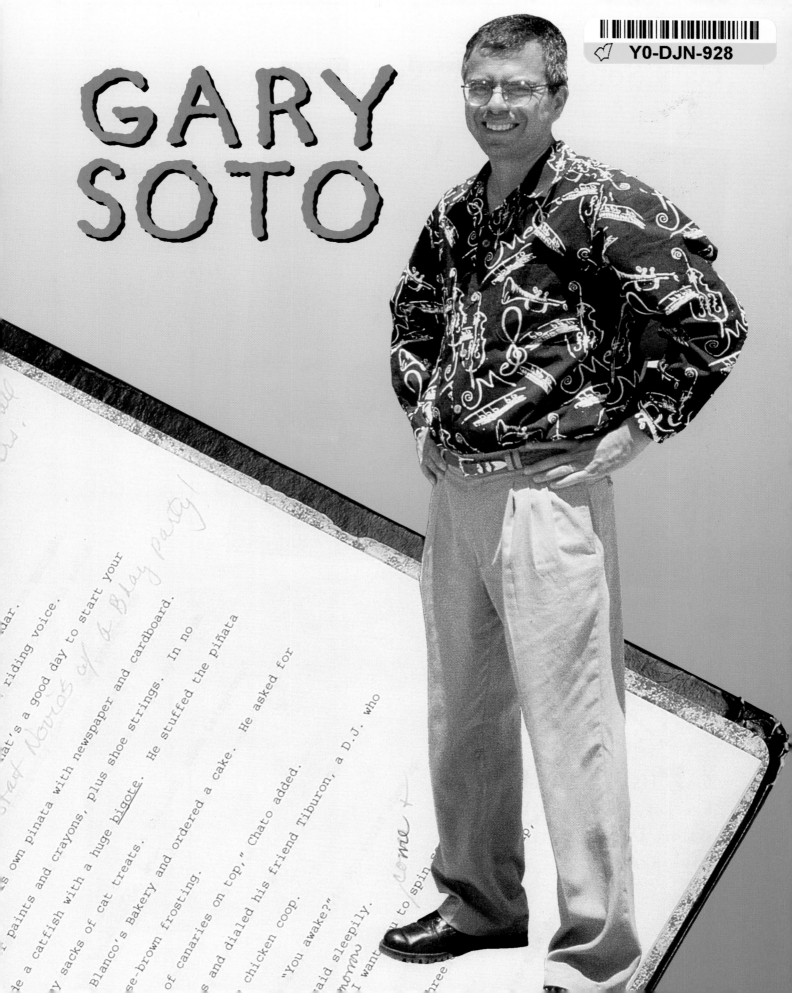

Gary Soto writes books and poems.

Gary was born in Fresno, California. Here he is on the front porch with his friends.

This is Gary.

Gary (far right) with his brother, Rick, and his sister, Debra, in their backyard

Gary read some poetry in college.
"This is great!" he thought.

Here Gary cools off
with his brother
and sister.

This is Gary's
report card from
third grade.

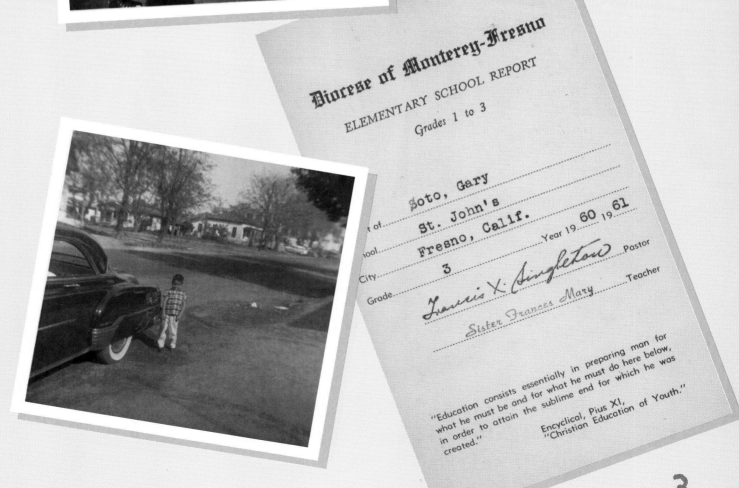

Diocese of Monterey-Fresno

ELEMENTARY SCHOOL REPORT

Grades 1 to 3

of .... Soto, Gary

ool. .... St. John's

City. .... Fresno, Calif.   Year 19 60 19 61

Grade. 3   *Francis X. Singleton*   Pastor

Sister Frances Mary .... Teacher

"Education consists essentially in preparing man for
what he must be and for what he must do here below,
in order to attain the sublime end for which he was
created."
                              Encyclical, Pius XI,
                              "Christian Education of Youth."

So Gary wrote his own poetry.

This is how Gary looked when he was twenty-one. He was writing poetry.

Gary likes to write in bed. Sometimes he uses a laptop computer.

Then Gary decided to write stories.

Gary's grandmother, Apolonia Soto, and Gary's grandfather, Francisco Soto, were both born in Mexico.

Gary wrote about his family and friends. This is Gary with his daughter, Mariko.

In his book, *Too Many Tamales,* Gary tells about a little girl. Gary has written many stories and poems for children and grown-ups.

Gary traveled to France. He was surprised to find a book he had written being sold in a French bookstore.

Gary is curious about many things. He enjoys going to museums. Here Gary is visiting an aviation museum.

Gary remembers things about growing up. Then he writes about them.

Gary visits many schools and meets a lot of children. Gary gets many letters, too. Here are two of them.

Dear Gary Soto,
Hello! My name is Belia. I am 12 years old. I really enjoy your books because they have a little bit of our culture, and I really like the words in Spanish. The book, *Pacific Crossing* was great! I really enjoyed it because I'm Mexican and I take Kempo Karate like Lincoln. I also agree with Lincoln about Kempo being very tiring. I am a purple belt in kempo going on blue belt. I also like all of your poems like "Oranges", I like it because it has a lot of details and it is very sweet. You are one of my favorite authors. Thank you for taking time to read this letter.

Always,
Belia
Belia

P.S.
Your books are great! I hope you write back soon.

Dear Mr. Soto,
Thank you for visiting ou school on the date of October 3, 1995.
I really enjoyed your prese for us. I liked "La Bamba" the best. My nephew, whom is 4, heard "La Cocaracha", and when I told him what it meant, he laughed. So, if you ever visit little kids' schools, maybe you can sing that and tell them what it means.
I always thought that writers were smart people too unwise to realize a joke or listen to music. Seeing you, and how you acted, changed my mind. You listen to music, told jokes, and were smart. I like a person like that.

Sincerely,
Matthew

7

Gary has won awards for writing.
He says, "Read as much as you can!"

Gary used to teach karate.

Let's Explore!

Gary Soto was born in Fresno, California. Trace a path from Fresno to Berkeley. In which direction would you go?

What Do You Think?

Reading Poetry

Share a poem you like. Write about what the poem means to you.

Be a Poet!

Gary Soto is a poet. Write a poem of your own. Then draw a picture to go with your poem.

My bike is new.
It's fast and fun.
I race up hills
To catch the sun.

IDEAS! IDEAS!

Gary Soto wrote about things he did as a child. Make a list of some things you could write about. Pick one and write a story about it.

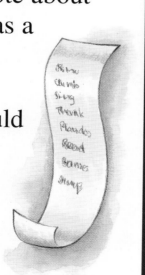

Interview the Writer

Suppose Gary Soto visited your classroom. What would you like to know about him? Make a list of questions you would ask.

Welcome, Gary

Meet Corky!

Gary Soto likes animals. One of his most special friends is his cat, Corky. Here Gary and Corky spend the morning together.

Reading the newspaper

Corky's favorite breakfast is a hot bowl of oatmeal! Gary likes it, too.

And now it's time to play!

Key Events

1952 Gary Soto was born in Fresno, California.

1974 He graduated from California State University.

1975 He married Carolyn Oda.

1977 Gary's first book of poetry was published.

1985 Gary's first book of short stories was published.